MUNSCH
Mini-Treasury Three

by Robert Munsch
art by Michael Martchenko
and Hélène Desputeaux

annick press
toronto • new york • vancouver

Cover illustration by Michael Martchenko

We acknowledge the support of the Canada Council for the Arts, the Ontario Arts Council, and the Government of Canada through the Canada Book Fund (CBF) for our publishing activities.

Cataloging in Publication
Munsch, Robert N., 1945-
[Novels. Selections]
    Munsch mini-treasury. Three / Robert Munsch ; Michael Martchenko, Helene Desputeaux.

Contents: Mortimer — Purple, green, and yellow — Show and tell
    — Something good — David's father.
ISBN 978-1-55451-651-3 (bound)

    I. Desputeaux, Hélène, illustrator II. Martchenko, Michael, illustrator III. Title. IV. Title: David's father. V. Title: Mortimer. VI. Title: Something good. VII. Title: Show and tell. VIII. Title: Purple, green and yellow.

PS8576.U575A6 2014   jC813'.54   C2013-907420-1

Distributed in Canada by:
Firefly Books Ltd.
50 Staples Avenue, Unit 1
Richmond Hill, ON
L4B 0A7

Published in the U.S.A. by Annick Press (U.S.) Ltd.
Distributed in the U.S.A. by:
Firefly Books (U.S.) Inc.
P.O. Box 1338, Ellicott Station
Buffalo, NY 14205

Printed and bound in China.

visit us at: **www.annickpress.com**
visit Robert Munsch at: **www.robertmunsch.com**

CONTENTS

MORTIMER

STORY • ROBERT MUNSCH

ART • MICHAEL MARTCHENKO

Where did This STory come from?

Mortimer was the first story Robert Munsch ever made up. It was 1971 and he was a student teacher at a nursery school. When he was asked to do circle time, he told a story about a little boy who didn't want to go to bed. He gave all the kids noisemakers so that when it came time to yell, "Clang, clang, rattle-bing-bang," they made an incredible racket. He told the story for years and years before he wrote it down and it became a book.

To Billy,
Sheila, and
Kathleen
Cronin

One night Mortimer's mother took him upstairs to go to bed—

thump
thump
thump
thump
thump
thump.

When they got upstairs Mortimer's mother opened the door to his room.

She threw him into bed and said,

"MORTIMER, BE QUIET."

Mortimer shook his head, yes.

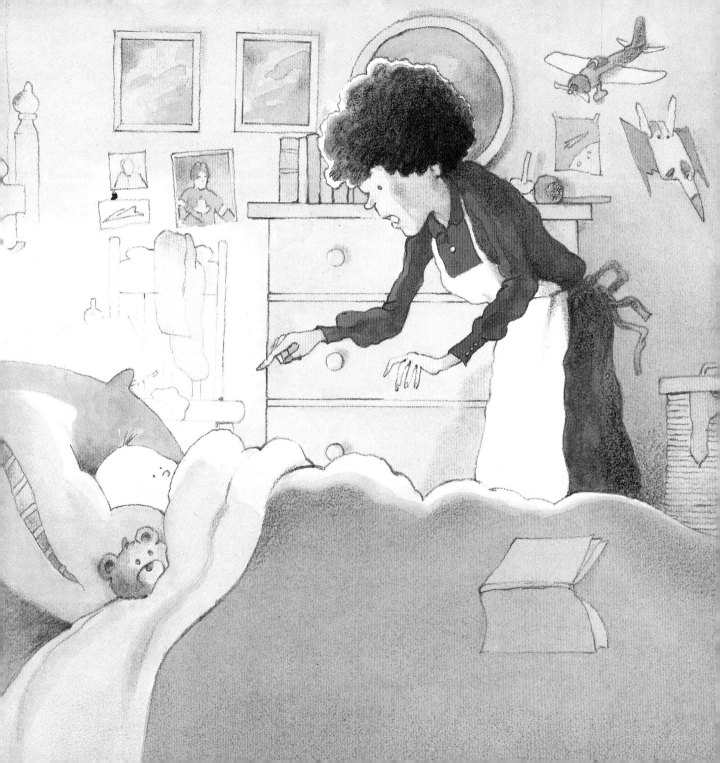

The mother shut the door.
Then she went back down the stairs—
thump thump thump thump thump.

As soon as she got back downstairs
Mortimer sang,

Clang, clang, rattle-bing-bang
Gonna make my noise all day.
Clang, clang, rattle-bing-bang
Gonna make my noise all day.

Mortimer's father heard all that noise.
He came up the stairs—

thump
thump
thump
thump
thump.

He opened the door and yelled,

"MORTIMER, BE QUIET."

Mortimer shook his head, yes.

The father went back down the stairs—
thump
   thump
       thump
           thump
               thump.

As soon as he got to the bottom of the
stairs Mortimer sang,

Clang, clang, rattle-bing-bang
Gonna make my noise all day.
Clang, clang, rattle-bing-bang
Gonna make my noise all day.

All of Mortimer's seventeen brothers
and sisters heard that noise, and they
all came up the stairs—

thump
thump
thump
thump
thump
thump.

They opened the door and yelled in a
tremendous, loud voice,

"MORTIMER, BE QUIET."

Mortimer shook his head, yes.

The brothers and sisters shut the door
and went downstairs—
thump_{thump}_{thump}_{thump}_{thump.}

As soon as they got to the bottom of
the stairs Mortimer sang,

> Clang, clang, rattle-bing-bang
> Gonna make my noise all day.
> Clang, clang, rattle-bing-bang
> Gonna make my noise all day.

They got so upset that they called the police. Two policemen came and they walked very slowly up the stairs—

thump.

thump

thump

thump

thump

thump

They opened the door and said in very deep, policemen-type voices,

"MORTIMER, BE QUIET."

The policemen shut the door and went
back down the stairs—
thump_{thump}_{thump}_{thump}_{thump.}

As soon as they got to the bottom of
the stairs Mortimer sang,

> Clang, clang, rattle-bing-bang
> Gonna make my noise all day.
> Clang, clang, rattle-bing-bang
> Gonna make my noise all day.

Well, downstairs no one knew what to do.
The mother got into a big fight with the policemen.
The father got into a big fight with the brothers and sisters.

Upstairs, Mortimer got so tired waiting for someone to come up that he fell asleep.

Purple, Green and Yellow

story by
Robert Munsch

illustrated by
Hélène Desputeaux

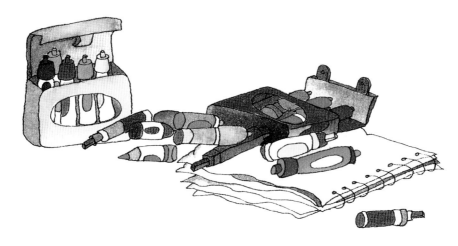

Where did This Story come from?

The idea for this book came in 1990, during a storytelling festival in Toronto. Robert Munsch found himself sitting beside a girl named Brigid, who was coloring her nails purple. He asked her if she liked to color with magic markers, and she said she certainly did! When it was his turn, Munsch got up in front of a room full of people and told the story *Purple, Green and Yellow*. The story remained virtually unchanged when it was turned into a book.

To Brigid Thurgood, Toronto, Ontario — R.M.
To Pénélope Link — H.D.

Brigid went to her mother and said, "I need some coloring markers. All my friends have coloring markers. They draw wonderful pictures. Mommy, I need some coloring markers."

"Oh, no!" said her mother. "I've heard about those coloring markers. Kids draw on walls, they draw on the floor, they draw on themselves. You can't have any coloring markers."

"Well," said Brigid, "there are these new coloring markers. They wash off with just water. I can't get into any trouble with coloring markers that wash off. Get me some of those."

"Well," said her mother, "all right."

So her mother went out and got Brigid 500 washable coloring markers.

Brigid went up to her room and drew wonderful pictures. She drew lemons that were yellower than lemons, and roses that were redder than roses, and oranges that were oranger than oranges.

Her mother was amazed.
She said, "Wow! My kid is an artist."

But after a week Brigid got bored. She went to her mother and said, "Mom, did I draw on the wall?"

"Nnnnooo," said her mother.
"Did I draw on the floor?"
"Nnnnooo," said her mother.
"Did I draw on myself?"
"Nnnnooo," said her mother.

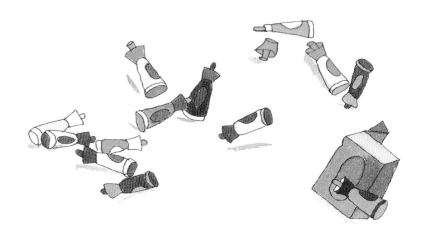

66 **W**ell," said Brigid, "I didn't get into any trouble and I need some new coloring markers. All my friends have them. Mommy, there are coloring markers that smell. They have ones that smell like roses and lemons and oranges and even ones that smell like cow plops. Mom, they have coloring markers that smell like anything you want! Mom, I need those coloring markers."

Her mother went out and got 500 coloring markers that smelled. Then Brigid went upstairs and she drew pictures. She drew lemons that smelled like lemons, and roses that smelled like roses, and oranges that smelled like oranges, and cow plops that smelled like cow plops.

Her mother said, "Wow! My kid is an artist."

ut after a week Brigid got bored. She said, "Mom, did I draw on the floor?"

"Nnnnooo," said her mother.
"Did I draw on the walls?"
"Nnnnooo," said her mother.
"Did I draw on myself?"
"Nnnnooo," said her mother.

"Well," said Brigid, "I need some new coloring markers. These are the best kind. All my friends have them. They are super-indelible-never-come-off-till-you're-dead-and-maybe-even-later coloring markers. Mom, I need them."

So her mother went out and got 500 super-indelible-never-come-off-till-you're-dead-and-maybe-even-later coloring markers. Brigid took them and drew pictures for three weeks. She drew lemons that looked better than lemons, and roses that looked better than roses and oranges that looked better than oranges and sunsets that looked better than sunsets.

hen she got bored.
She said, "I'm tired of drawing on the paper. But I am not going to draw on the walls and I am not going to draw on the floor and I'm not going to draw on myself — but everybody knows it's okay to color your fingernails. Even my mother colors her fingernails."

So Brigid took a purple super-indelible-never-come-off-till-you're-dead-and-maybe-even-later coloring marker, and she colored her thumbnail bright purple.

And that was so pretty, she colored all her fingernails purple, black and yellow.

And that was so pretty, she colored her hands yellow, green and red.

45

And that was so pretty,
she colored her face purple,
green, yellow and blue.

And that was so pretty,
she colored her belly-button
blue.

And that was so pretty, she colored herself all sorts of colors almost entirely all over.

Then Brigid looked in the mirror and said, "What have I done! My mother is going to kill me." So she ran into the bathroom and washed her hands for half an hour. Nothing came off. Her hands still looked like mixed-up rainbows.

Then she had a wonderful idea.

She reached way down into the bottom of the coloring markers and got a special-colored marker. It was the same color she was. She took that marker and colored herself all over until she was her regular color again. In fact, she looked even better than before — almost too good to be true.

She went downstairs and her mother said, "Why, Brigid, you're looking really good today."

"Right," said Brigid.

Then her mother said, "It's time to wash your hands for dinner."

But Brigid was afraid that the special color would not stick to the colors underneath, so she said, "I already washed my hands."

But her mother smelled her hands and said, "Ahhh. No soap!" She took Brigid into the bathroom and washed her hands and face. All the special color came off and Brigid looked like mixed-up rainbows.

"Oh, no!" said her mother. "Brigid, did you color your hands with the coloring markers that wash off?"

"Nnnnooo."

"Brigid, did you color your hands with the coloring markers that smell?"

"Nnnnnooooo."

"Did you use the super-indelible-never-come-off-till-you're-dead-and-maybe-even-later coloring markers?"

"Yes!"

"Yikes!" yelled her mother.

S he called the doctor and said, "HELP! HELP! HELP! My daughter has colored herself with super-indelible-never-come-off-till-you're-dead-and-maybe-even-later coloring markers."

"Oh, dear," said the doctor. "Sometimes they never come off."

The doctor came over and gave Brigid a large, orange pill. She said, "Take this pill, wait five minutes and then take a bath."

So Brigid took the pill, waited five minutes, and jumped into the bathtub. Her mother stood outside the door and yelled, "Is it working? Is it working?"

"Yes," said Brigid. "Everything is coming off." And Brigid was right, everything had come off. When Brigid walked out of the bathroom she was invisible.

"Oh, no," yelled her mother. "You can't go to school if you're invisible. You can't go to university if you're invisible. You'll never get a job if you're invisible. Brigid, you've wrecked your life!"

"**D**on't worry," said Brigid. She ran into her room, got the special-colored marker and colored herself entirely all over until you couldn't tell the difference. In fact, she looked even better than before — almost too good to be true.

But her mother said, "Brigid, you can't go through life like that. You're just a picture. Everyone will know there is something wrong."

"No they won't," said Brigid.

"Yes they will," said her mother.

"No they won't," said Brigid. "I colored Daddy while he was taking a nap and you haven't noticed anything yet!"

"Good heavens!" yelled her mother, and she ran into the living-room and looked at Daddy. He looked even better than before — almost too good to be true.

"Doesn't he look great?" asked Brigid.

"I couldn't even tell the difference," said her mother.

"Right," said Brigid, "and neither will he...

s long as he doesn't get wet."

Show and Tell

by Robert Munsch
illustrations by Michael Martchenko

Where did This Story come from?

Robert Munsch was visiting a school in Gander, Newfoundland, when he asked the kids to help him make up a story. The story they came up with was about finding a baby in the school. He told it over and over again until finally, it got mixed up with another story about a little girl who went to a doctor and the doctor kept trying to stick her with bigger and bigger needles.

to Ben and Sharon Chia, Guelph, Ont.

Benjamin wanted to take something really neat to school for show and tell, so he decided to take his new baby sister. He went upstairs, picked her up, put her in his knapsack and walked off to school.

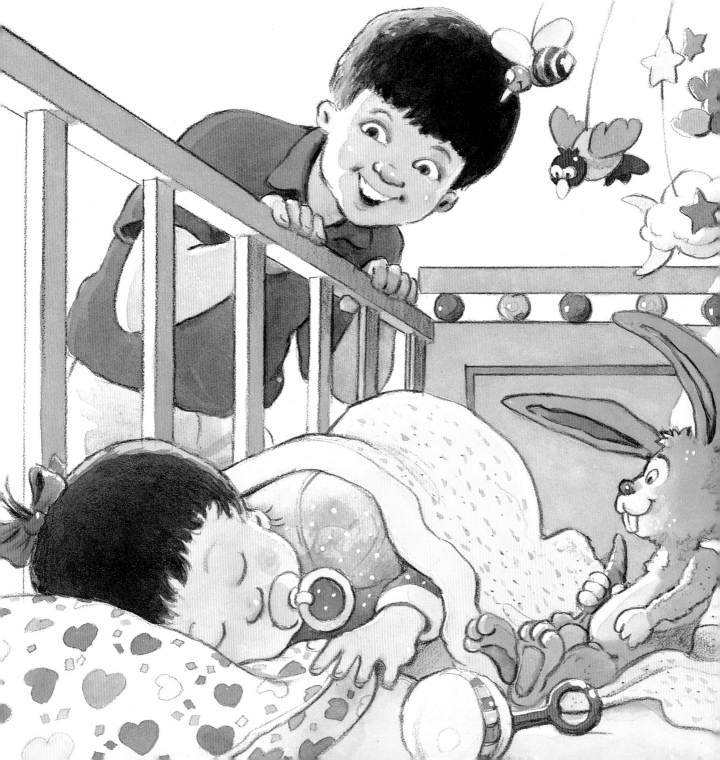

But when Ben sat down, his baby sister finally woke up. She was not happy inside the knapsack and started to cry: "WAAA, WAAA, WAAA, WAAA, WAAA."

The teacher looked at him and said, "Benjamin, stop making that noise."

Ben said, "That's not me. It's my baby sister. She's in my knapsack. I brought her for show and tell."

"Yikes!" said the teacher. "You can't keep a baby in a knapsack!" She grabbed Ben's knapsack and opened it up. The baby looked at the teacher and said, "WAAA, WAAA, WAAA, WAAA, WAAA."

"Don't worry," said the teacher. "I know how to take care of babies." She picked it up and rocked it back and forth, back and forth, back and forth.

Unfortunately, the teacher was not the baby's mother and she didn't rock quite right. The baby cried even louder: "WAAA, WAAA, WAAA, WAAA, WAAA."

The principal came running in. He looked at the teacher and said, "Stop making that noise!"

The teacher said, "It's not me. It's Sharon, Ben's new baby sister. He brought her for show and tell. She won't shut up!"

The principal said, "Ah, don't worry. I know how to make kids be quiet." He picked up the baby and yelled, "HEY, YOU! BE QUIET!" The baby did not like that at all. It screamed, really loudly, "WAAA, WAAA, WAAA, WAAA, WAAA."

The principal said, "What's the matter with this baby? It must be sick. I'll call a doctor."

The doctor came with a big black bag. She looked in the baby's eyes and she looked in the baby's ears and she looked in the baby's mouth. She said, "Ah! Don't worry. I know what to do. This baby needs a needle!"

So the doctor opened her bag, got out a short needle and said, "Naaaah, TOO SMALL."

The doctor opened her bag, got out a longer needle and said, "Naaaah, TOO SMALL."

The doctor opened her bag, got out a really long needle and said, "Naaaah, TOO SMALL."

The doctor reached into her bag, got out an enormous needle and said, "Ahhh, JUST RIGHT."

When the baby saw that enormous needle, it yelled, as loudly as it could, "WAAA, WAAA, WAAA, WAAA, WAAA."

Ben said, "What's the matter with this school? Nobody knows what to do with a baby." He ran down to the principal's office and called his mother on the phone. He said, "HELP, HELP, HELP! You have to come to school right away."

The mother said, "Ben, your little sister is lost! I can't come to school. I have to find her."

"She's not lost," said Ben. "I took her to school in my knapsack."

"Oh, no!" yelled the mother. She ran down the street and into the school. The principal and the teacher and the doctor were standing around the baby, and the baby was yelling, as loudly as possible, "WAAA, WAAA, WAAA, WAAA, WAAA."

The mother picked up the baby and rocked it back and forth, back and forth, back and forth. The baby said, "Ahhhhhhhhh," and went to sleep.

"Oh, thank you! Oh, thank you!" said the principal. "That baby was making so much noise, it was just making me feel sick!"

"SICK?" said the doctor. "SICK! Did that man say he was SICK? He must need a needle." So the doctor opened her bag, got out a short needle and said, "Naaaah, TOO SMALL."

The doctor opened her bag, got out a longer needle and said, "Naaaah, TOO SMALL."

The doctor opened her bag, got out a really long needle and said, "Naaaah, TOO SMALL."

The doctor reached into her bag, got out an enormous needle and said, "Ahhh, JUST RIGHT."

The principal looked at that enormous needle and said, "WAAA, WAAA, WAAA, WAAA, WAAA," and ran out the door.

"Now," said the mother, "it's time to take this baby home."

"Right," said Ben. "You can use my knapsack."

"What a good idea," said the mother.

Ben and his mother put the baby into bed.
She went to sleep and didn't cry, not even once.

Ben went back to school carrying some strange things for show and tell.

And he wasn't out of place at all ...

SOMETHING GOOD

Story by Robert Munsch
Art by Michael Martchenko

Where did This Story come from?

This story evolved from a trip Robert Munsch took to the supermarket, where he noticed a little girl sitting so still in her mother's cart that he thought, "She could almost be a doll." The doll idea stayed in his head, and eventually it turned into the story *Something Good.* The kids in the book are his own, and Munsch's wife appears on the last page. The father who always gets mad at the little kid for asking for all the sugary food is modeled on himself.

★ ★ ★

*To Tyya, Andrew, Julie
    and Ann Munsch
Guelph, Ontario*

Tyya went shopping with her father and her brother and her sister. She pushed the cart up the aisle and down the aisle, up the aisle and down the aisle, up the aisle and down the aisle.

Tyya said, "Sometimes my father doesn't buy good food. He gets bread, eggs, milk, cheese, spinach—nothing any good! He doesn't buy ICE CREAM! COOKIES! CHOCOLATE BARS! or GINGER ALE!"

So Tyya very quietly snuck away from her father and got a cart of her own. She pushed it over to the ice cream. Then she put one hundred boxes of ice cream into her cart.

Tyya pushed that cart up behind her father and said, "DADDY, LOOK!" Her father turned around and yelled, "YIKES!"

Tyya said, "DADDY! GOOD FOOD!"

"Oh, no," said her father. "This is sugary junk. It will rot your teeth. It will lower your IQ. Put it ALL BACK!"

So Tyya put back the one hundred boxes of ice cream. She meant to go right back to her father, but on the way she had to pass the candy. She put three hundred chocolate bars into her cart.

Tyya pushed that cart up behind her father and said, "DADDY, LOOK!" Her father turned around and said, "YIKES!"

Tyya said, "DADDY! GOOD FOOD!"

"Oh, no," said her father. "This is sugary junk. Put it ALL BACK!" So Tyya put back all the chocolate bars. Then her father said, "Okay, Tyya, I have had it. You stand here and DON'T MOVE."

Tyya knew she was in BIG trouble, so she stood there and DIDN'T MOVE. Some friends came by and said hello. Tyya didn't move. A man ran over her toe with his cart. Tyya still didn't move.

A lady who worked at the store came by and looked at Tyya. She looked her over from the top down, and she looked her over from the bottom up. She knocked Tyya on the head—and Tyya still didn't move.

The lady said, "This is the nicest doll I have ever seen. It looks almost real." She put a price tag on Tyya's nose that said $29.95. Then she picked Tyya up and put her on the shelf with all the other dolls.

A man came along and looked at Tyya. He said, "This is the nicest doll I have ever seen. I'm going to get that doll for my son." He picked up Tyya by the hair.

Tyya yelled, very loudly, "STOP."

The man screamed, "EYAAAAH! IT'S ALIVE!" And he ran down the aisle, knocking over a pile of five hundred apples.

A lady came along and looked at Tyya. She said, "This is the nicest doll I have ever seen. I think I will buy this doll for my daughter." She picked up Tyya by the ear. Tyya yelled, as loudly as she could, "STOP."

The lady screamed, "EYAAAAH! IT'S ALIVE!" And she ran down the aisle, knocking over a pile of five hundred oranges.

Then Tyya's father came along, looking for his daughter. He said, "Tyya? Tyya? Tyya? Tyya? Where are you? ... TYYA! What are you doing on that shelf?"

Tyya said, "It's all your fault. You told me not to move and people are trying to buy me, WAAAAAHHHHH!"

"Oh, come now," said her father. "I won't let anybody buy you." He gave Tyya a big kiss and a big hug; then they went to pay for all the food.

The man at the cash register looked at Tyya and said, "Hey, Mister, you can't take that kid out of the store. You have to pay for her. It says so right on her nose: twenty-nine ninety-five."

"Wait," said the father. "This is my own kid. I don't have to pay for my own kid."

The man said, "If it has a price tag, you have to pay for it."

"I won't pay," said the father.

"You've got to," said the man.

The father said, "NNNNO."

The man said, "YYYYES."

The father said, "NNNNO!"

The man said, "YYYYES!"

The father and Andrew and Julie all yelled, "NNNNNNO!"

Then Tyya quietly said, "Daddy, don't you think I'm worth twenty-nine ninety-five?"

"Ah...Um...I mean... Well, of course you're worth twenty-nine ninety-five," said the father. He reached into his wallet, got out the money, paid the man, and took the price tag off Tyya's nose.

Tyya gave her father a big kiss, SMMMER-CCHH, and a big hug, MMMMMMMMMM, and then she said, "Daddy, you finally bought something good after all."

Then her father picked up Tyya and gave her a big long hug—and didn't say anything at all.

DAVID'S FATHER

Story
by Robert N. Munsch

Art
Michael Martchenko

Where did this story come from?

Robert Munsch and his wife adopted their second child, Julie, when she was five and a half years old. Every night, he would tell her stories before she went to bed. One day, she asked for a story about a girl who was afraid to meet new people, and an adopted boy who didn't look like his father. The result, *David's Father*, was the longest running bedtime story ever: Munsch told it to Julie every night for four months.

★ ★ ★

To Julie

Julie was skipping home from school. She came to a large moving van. A man came out carrying a spoon—only it was as big as a shovel. Another man came out carrying a fork—only it was as big as a pitchfork. A third man came out carrying a knife—only it was as big as a flagpole.

"Yikes," said Julie, "I don't want to get to know these people at all."

She ran all the way home and hid under her bed till dinner time.

The next day Julie was skipping home from school again. A boy was standing where the moving van had been. He said, "Hi, my name's David. Would you like to come and play?" Julie looked at him very carefully. He seemed to be a regular sort of boy, so she stayed to play.

At five o'clock, from far away down the street, someone called, "Julie, come and eat."

"That's my mother," said Julie. Then someone called, ***"DAVID!!!"***

"That's my father," said David.

Julie jumped up in the air, ran around in a circle three times, ran home and locked herself in her room till it was time for breakfast the next morning.

The next day Julie was skipping home and she saw David again. He said, "Hi, Julie, do you want to come and play?" Julie looked at him very, very carefully. He seemed to be a regular boy, so she stayed and played.

When it was almost five o'clock, David said, "Julie, please stay for dinner."

But Julie remembered the big knife, the big fork and the big spoon. "Well, I don't know," she said, "maybe it's a bad idea. I think maybe no. Good-bye, good-bye, good-bye."

"Well," said David, "we're having cheeseburgers, chocolate milk shakes and a salad."

"Oh?" said Julie, "I love cheeseburgers. I'll stay, I'll stay."

So they went into the kitchen. There was a small table with cheeseburgers, milk shakes and salads. On the other side of the room there was an enormous table. On it were a spoon as big as a shovel, a fork as big as a pitchfork and a knife as big as a flagpole. "David," whispered Julie, "who sits there?"

"Oh," said David. "That's where my father sits. You can hear him coming now." David's father sounded like this:

broum broum broum

He opened the door.

David's father was a giant. On his table there were 26 snails, three fried octopuses and 16 bricks covered with chocolate sauce.

David and Julie ate their cheeseburgers and the father ate the snails. David and Julie drank their milk shakes and the father ate the fried octopuses. David and Julie ate their salads and the father ate his chocolate-covered bricks.

David's father asked Julie if she would like a snail.
Julie said no. David's father asked Julie if she would like
an octopus. Julie said no. David's father asked Julie if she
would like a delicious chocolate-covered brick. Julie said,
"No, but please, may I have another milk shake?" So
David's father made her another milk shake.

When they were done Julie said, very softly so the father couldn't hear, "David, you don't look very much like your father."

"Well, I'm adopted," said David.

"Oh," said Julie. "Well, do you like your father?"

"He's great," said David, "come for a walk and see."

So they walked down the street. Julie and David skipped, and the father went

broum broum broum.

They came to a road and they couldn't get across. The cars would not stop for David. The cars would not stop for Julie. The father walked into the middle of the road, looked at the cars and yelled,

"stop."

The cars all jumped up into the air, ran around in a circle three times and went back up the street so fast they forgot their tires.

Julie and David crossed the street and went into a store. The man who ran the store didn't like serving kids. They waited five minutes, 10 minutes, 15 minutes. Then David's father came in. He looked at the storekeeper and said, **"*THESE KIDS ARE MY FRIENDS!*"** The man jumped up into the air, ran around the store three times and gave David and Julie three boxes of ice cream, 11 bags of potato chips and 19 life savers, all for free. Julie and David walked down the street and went around a bend.

There were six big kids from grade eight standing in the middle of the sidewalk. They looked at David. They looked at Julie and they looked at the food. Then one big kid reached down and grabbed a box of ice cream. David's father came round the bend. He looked at the big kids and yelled,

"beat it."

They jumped right out of their shirts. They jumped right out of their pants and ran down the street in their underwear. Julie ran after them, but she slipped and scraped her elbow.

David's father picked her up and held her. Then he put a special giant bandage on her elbow.

Julie said, "Well, David, you do have a very nice father after all, but he is still kind of scary."

"You think he is scary?" said David. "Wait till you meet my grandmother."

Books in the Munsch for Kids series:

The Dark
Mud Puddle
The Paper Bag Princess
The Boy in the Drawer
Jonathan Cleaned Up, Then He Heard a Sound
Murmel, Murmel, Murmel
Millicent and the Wind
Mortimer
The Fire Station
Angela's Airplane
David's Father
Thomas' Snowsuit
50 Below Zero
I Have to Go!
Moira's Birthday
A Promise is a Promise
Pigs
Something Good
Show and Tell
Purple, Green and Yellow
Wait and See
Where is Gah-Ning?
From Far Away
Stephanie's Ponytail
Munschworks
Munschworks 2
Munschworks 3
Munschworks 4
The Munschworks Grand Treasury
Munsch Mini-Treasury One
Munsch Mini-Treasury Two

For information on these titles please visit www.annickpress.com
Many Munsch titles are available in French and/or Spanish, as well as in
board book and e-book editions. Please contact your favorite supplier.